FRANKLIN PARK PUBLIC LIBRARY

W9-AXP-711

Daddy Is a Cozy Hug

Rhonda Gowler Greene
illustrated by Maggie Smith

Walker & Company
New York

First published in the United States of America in May 2010 by
Walker Publishing Company, Inc., a division of Bloomsbury Publishing, Inc.
Visit Walker & Company's Web site at www.bloomsburykids.com

For information about permission to reproduce selections from this book, write to
Permissions, Walker & Company, 175 Fifth Avenue, New York, New York 10010

Library of Congress Cataloging-in-Publication Data
Greene, Rhonda Gowler.
Daddy is a cozy hug / Rhonda Gowler Greene ; illustrated by Maggie Smith.
p. cm.
Summary: A child celebrates all of the wonderful things a father can be throughout the year, from a wiggling fish in summer to a warm blanket in winter.
ISBN-13: 978-0-8027-9728-5 • ISBN-10: 0-8027-9728-8
[1. Stories in rhyme. 2. Father and child—Fiction. 3. Seasons—Fiction. 4. Year—Fiction.] I. Smith, Maggie, ill. II. Title.
PZ8.3.G824Dad 2010 [E]—dc22 2008013357

Book design by Nicole Gastonguay
Typeset in Sassoon Sans
Art created with watercolors and acrylics on 140-lb cold-pressed paper

Printed in China by L. Rex Printing Co. Ltd., Dongguan, Guangdong
2 4 6 8 10 9 7 5 3 1

All papers used by Walker & Company are natural, recyclable products made from wood grown in well-managed forests. The manufacturing processes conform to the environmental regulations of the country of origin.

In memory of Dad and all his cozy hugs,

and for Gary, with love —R. G. G.

For Graham and his daddy, Duncan

—M. S.

Daddy is a fish with fins when summer heats the air.

We *splish* and *splash* in crashing waves—
a wiggling, wriggling pair.

Daddy is a *tap-tap* hammer,

building things with me.

We work *tap-tap* and make a house

for birdies in our tree.

Daddy is my pillow where I rest my sleepy head.

When camping far

beneath the stars, he's better than a bed.

Daddy is a sneaky fox

when playing hide-and-seek.

He makes himself so hard to find . . .

I sometimes have to peek.

Daddy is a handy horse for cowpokes on the go.

He bucks and snorts,

then giddyups . . .

until I tell him, “Whoa!”

Daddy is a pile of leaves
when fall comes rolling round.

One,
two,
three . . .
I run and—jump!
We make a crunchy sound!

Chugga-chugga
chugga-chugga

Daddy is a choo-choo train that *clickity-clacks* along.
With me as engineer up front, we sing a chugging song.

CHOO-CHOO!

Daddy is my blanket when cold winds begin to blow.

Bundled round me soft and snug,

he warms me from the snow.

Daddy is my valentine

with sticky, gummy glue,

sprinkled with a

glitter message—

I LOVE YOU.

Daddy is the rushing wind
that makes my kite
take wing . . .

and dip and dive, as if alive, a-dancing on a string.

Daddy's my umbrella
that hides me from drip-drops.
He keeps me dry from cloudy skies
until the spring rain stops.

me
to Grand

Daddy is a cozy hug when tucking me in tight.

He kisses me on cheek—*and nose*—

then whispers, "Nighty-night."

Daddy is so many things with me

the whole year through.

I'm glad I have my daddy . . .

Daddy,
I love you.